The ~~Ferocious~~ CHOCOLATE Wolf

By Lizzie Finlay

FIVE

MEDWAY LIBRARIES

9560000155807

Medway Libraries and Archives	
9560000155807	
Askews & Holts	
	£6.99
	TWY

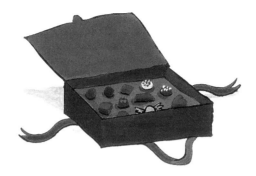

For Heather & Tony,
who both enjoy
a chocolate! X

THE FEROCIOUS CHOCOLATE WOLF

First published in Great Britain in 2020 by Five Quills
93 Oakwood Court, London W14 8JZ
www.fivequills.co.uk
Five Quills and associated logos are trademarks of Five Quills Ltd.

Text and illustrations copyright © 2020 Lizzie Finlay
The right of Lizzie Finlay to be identified as the author and illustrator of this work has been asserted.
Edited by Natascha Biebow at Blue Elephant Storyshaping
Designed by Cathy Tincknell

All rights reserved. No part of this publication may be reproduced,
stored in or introduced to a retrieval system, or transmitted, in any
form or by any means (electronic, mechanical, photocopying,
recording or otherwise), without the prior written
permission of the publisher.

A CIP record for this title is available from
the British Library

ISBN 978-0-9935537-9-0

1 3 5 7 9 10 8 6 4 2

Printed in Croatia
by INK69

Ferocious was a very unusual sort of wolf.
He LOVED chocolate!

Ever since he was little, his dream was to make the finest chocolates in all the land.

Ferocious practised and practised. He melted, stirred and perfected his special chocolates,

until at last . . .

He was ready!

Ferocious stepped proudly out of his very own shop. "Roll up, roll up . . . Come and try my delicious chocolates!" he sang.

But a strange thing happened – everyone ran away!

CHOCOLATE SHOP OPEN

Eeek! It's the big bad wolf!

Just look at those sharp teeth!

"How peculiar!" thought Ferocious. "Perhaps the animals have never tasted chocolate before?"

He decided to give out some samples for free.

But everyone ran away and hid again, except for . . .

. . . one brave Piggy, just back from the big city.

Before anyone could warn him, he trotted straight up to the WOLF.

All the animals held their breath.

"Would you like to try a Caramel Delight?" Ferocious asked.

Piggy closed his eyes and tasted it.

"Mmmm, scrumptious!"

"I know," whispered Ferocious. "Those are my favourites."

The animals waited until Ferocious
was gone, then crept out.

"You're lucky he didn't eat YOU!"
squawked Mrs Chicken.

"I'd stay away from that wolf
if I were you!"

Ferocious was delighted.

"Would you like to try today's special, the **Strawberry Sparkle?**"

Piggy did and it was DELICIOUS!

All day long, Piggy chatted to his new friend.

All day long, Ferocious waited for some more customers. But none came.

When Piggy bounced into the shop the next
morning, Ferocious looked miserable.

"No one will try my delicious
chocolates - except you!"

Piggy had a magical idea. "How about if I give some free chocolates to my friends? Then everyone will know how AMAZING they really are."

Ferocious could hardly speak. "You'd really do that for me?"

"TOTALLY!" said Piggy.

Everyone loved Ferocious' free chocolates
so much they ordered some
right away – all except for
Mrs Chicken.

Wolf
Chocolates –
NO WAY!

Piggy promised to deliver their orders
first thing the next day.

Ferocious mixed, melted and
moulded the special chocolates.
Piggy helped.

Early the next morning, they loaded the beautiful boxes carefully onto Piggy's bicycle. Ferocious frowned at the darkening sky. "It's starting to rain – you'd better hurry, Piggy!"

The rain whooshed down and a big storm blew up.

Piggy's bike skidded and BUMP!

The animals waited and waited
for their deliveries. But there was
no sign of the chocolates
OR of their friend Piggy!
There was a huge HULLABALLOO.

"You shouldn't have ordered chocolates from a WOLF! It was a trap!"

Mrs Chicken shrieked.

"Piggy's been eaten, I tell you!"

She organized a search party.
Benjie, his friend Archie and
two plucky ducks set off first.

"Be back by lunchtime!"
Mrs Chicken cried.

But at lunchtime, the rain splooshed down harder
and there was no sign of them OR of Piggy.

"We'll ALL have to go and look for them," Mrs Chicken clucked.

"I bet that wolf is eating chocolate-covered Piggy as we speak."

So the animals gathered their courage and set off into the cold, rainy afternoon. Filled with terror, they approached Ferocious' chocolate shop.

As they got closer, they heard laughter and the sound of clinking china.

"Probably a pack of wolves enjoying their feast!"

clucked Mrs Chicken.

They peeped through
the window . . .

There was Piggy safe and sound, and the WOLF was serving Benjie, Archie and the ducks 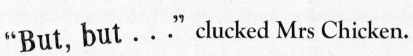!

"This is my friend Ferocious," Piggy said. "He rescued me!"

"But, but . . ." clucked Mrs Chicken.

"Come inside and warm up,"
offered Ferocious kindly.

Ferocious' hot chocolate was so moreish that even Mrs Chicken had to have seconds.

Ferocious promised to deliver the animals'
chocolate orders the very next day. Then he
treated them to a **mouth-watering** tour
of his shop.

No animals
got eaten . . .

Well, only chocolate ones!